I Love You, Dear Dragon

Modern Curriculum Press
**BEGINNING
TO
READ**
Series

I Love You, Dear Dragon

Margaret Hillert

Illustrated by Carl Kock

 MODERN CURRICULUM PRESS

Library of Congress Cataloging in Publication Data

Hillert, Margaret.
  I love you, dear dragon.

  (MCP beginning-to-read books)
  SUMMARY: A boy and his pet dragon celebrate Valentine's Day by noticing all the red things they see, making Valentines, and eating a Valentine cake.
  [1. St. Valentine's Day—Fiction. 2. Dragons—Fiction] I. Kock, Carl. II. Title.
PZ7.H558Ial   [E]   79–23669
ISBN 0-8136-5023-2 (Hardbound)
ISBN 0-8136-5523-4 (Paperback)

20 19 18 17 16 15 14 13 12 11   06 05 04 03 02 01 00

Red, red, red.
I like red.
Red is pretty.

5

Look up here.

Here is something red.

Little and red.

It is pretty.
It wants something to eat.
We can help it.

7

Oh, oh, oh.

Here is something red.

Something big, big and red.

Look at it go.
It can help.
It can do good work.

And look up here.
Look up, up, up.
This is red, too.

It can help us.
Do not go.
Look and look.

Now we can go.
Run, run, run.
But look out, too.

14

Here is something big and red.
I work in here.
I play here, too.

Here we are.

Mother wants something in here.

Something red.

We will look for it.

Can we find it?

Yes, yes.

This is it.

This is what we want.

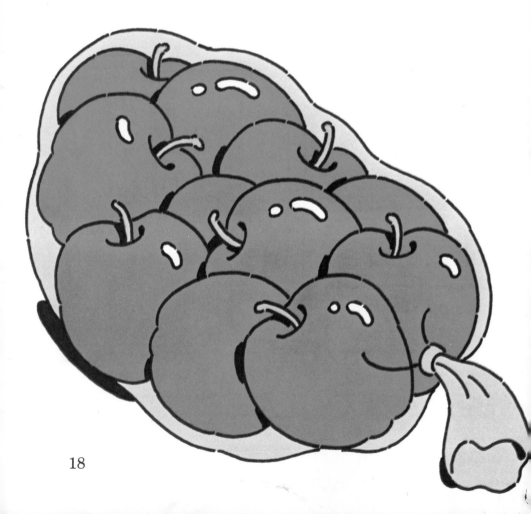

Mother, Mother.
Here we are.
Here is what you want.

19

Here is one for you to eat.
And here is one for you.
It is good for you and pretty, too.

21

Look who is here
with something for us.
What is it?
Guess what it is.

22

Oh, look at it.

It is pretty.

It is red.

"I love you" is on it.

We can make something like this.
Do it like this.
Work, work, work.

See here, Mother.
See what we can make.
Do you like it?

25

I do. I do.
But see what I can make for you.
26 Something to eat.

Oh, my.
This is good.
Good, good, good!
We like it.

And we like what Father can do.
This is fun.
Good fun for us.

Here you are with me.
And here I am with you.
I love you.
I love you, dear dragon.

31

Margaret Hillert, author of several books in the MCP Beginning-To-Read Series, is a writer, poet, and teacher.

I Love You, Dear Dragon uses the 60 words listed below.

am	father	make	see
and	find	man	something
are	for	me	
at	fun	mother	this
		my	to
big	go		too
but	good	not	
	guess	now	up
can			us
come(s)	help	oh	
	here	on	want(s)
dear		one	we
do	I	out	what
dragon	in		who
	is	play	will
eat	it	pretty	with
			work
	like	red	
	little	run	yes
	look		you
	love		